characters created by Lauren Child

But I AM an alligator

PUFFIN

Text based on the script written by Bridget Hurst

Illustrations from the TV animation produced by Tiger Aspect

PUFFIN BOOKS
Published by the Penguin Group: London, New York, Australia,
Canada, India, Ireland, New Zealand and South Africa
Penguin Books Ltd, Registered Offices: 80 Strand, London WC2R 0RL, England

puffinbooks.com

This edition published in Great Britain in Puffin Books 2010
1 3 5 7 9 8 6 4 2
Text and illustrations copyright © Lauren Child / Tiger Aspect Productions Limited, 2008
The Charlie and Lola Logo is a trademark of Lauren Child
All rights reserved. The moral right of the author/illustrator has been asserted
Manufactured in China
ISBN: 978-0-141-33492-9
This edition produced for The Book People Ltd,
Hall Wood Avenue, Haydock, St Helens, WA11 9UL

I have this little sister Lola.
She is small and very funny.
One thing Lola loves is **dressing** up.
"This is my favourite **fancy** dress **costume**
and I'm not ever NEVER taking it off," says Lola.

Then Lola says,
     "Did you know
all-i-gators live in
          swamps and rivers
where they are very
difficult to see?

That's because they are
          ca-moo-flarged.

And, you know,
alligators lay eggs,
          not babies.

"And sometimes they grow
BIGGER
than even our table!"
says Lola.

"So you see, Charlie,
alligators are really
very interesting.
That's why I am
going to wear my
alligator costume
ALL the time."

So I say,
"ALL the time, Lola?"

And she says,
"Yes, Charlie.
I'm not taking it off ever!
NEVER!"

When Mum takes us
    shopping, Lola says,
"I want to eat what
        all-i-gators eat."

I say,
"I don't think they eat
        frozen prawns, Lola."

But Lola shouts,
    "Oh, they absolutely
do, Charlie!
        Alligators LOVE
    frozen prawns!"

And I say,
"Shhh, Lola. Everyone's looking at us."

At the park,
Lola is STILL wearing her
    alligator costume.

Marv says,
    "Have you asked her
to take it off?"

So I say,
"A **gazillion**, million times,
        but she says
she is going to
        wear it FOREVER!"

And Marv says,
        "Well, she can't
wear it to **school**, can she?"

And I say, "NO! She
can't wear it to **school!**"

"Of course
I am going to wear it
        to **school**," says Lola.

And I say,
"I really don't think
        it's such a good idea.
Won't your friends
        think wearing
an **alligator costume**
        is a bit **strange**?"

Lola says,
        "No, Charlie.
I think they will all want
        alligator costumes,
too. Especially when
        I do my **talk**."

So I say,
"YOUR TALK?"

And Lola says,
"Yes, Charlie!
We have to do a talk in
assembly tomorrow.
It's called
'All About Me'."

Then I say,
"But you are
NOT an alligator, Lola.
Don't you think it
would be better
if you tell the whole
school about YOU,
dressed as YOU?
You could tell
them about...

"... how you like

drawing...

... and how you
always hop into bed...

... and how **pink milk** is your favourite and your best."

Lola says,
"That would not be very interesting. Everybody already knows I like **pink milk!**"

And so I say,
"I could help you with your **talk**, if you like."

But Lola says,
"I do not **need** any help."

At assembly the next day,
Lola says,
"My name is Lola,
and I like **dressing** up.

At the moment,
I like **dressing** up as
an **all-i-gator**
because it is my most
favourite costume
and it is my best.

I used to like **dressing** up as a Spanish lady.

Or sometimes as a circus person.

But I could also **dress** up as...

"... a doctor!

Or a caterpillar...

... who turns into a **butterfly**."

And the whole school says,
"**Wow!**"

Lola says,
"I love **dressing** up,
because I can be whatever
I want to be...
and that is my **best**."

Everyone cheers.

And I say,
"Well done, Lola!"

The next day,
Lola is not an **alligator**.
She has whiskers, pointy ears and a tail.
Lola says, "**Meow!**"
And I say, "Oh no."

Charlie has this little sister Lola.
She says, "Alligators are really very interesting.
That's why I am going to wear
my alligator costume ALL the time."
So Charlie asks, "ALL the time, Lola?"
And Lola says,
"Yes. I'm not taking it off ever! NEVER!"

Look out for **Boo! MADE you jump!**

and

and

I CAN do anything that's **everything** ALL on my **own**

This is ACTUALLY my Party

"An irresistibly comic duo" – *Sunday Telegraph*
"Wildly imaginative" – *Guardian*

tiger aspect

U.K. £4.99   CE

PUFFIN

ISBN 978-0-141-33492-9

9 780141 334929

puffinbooks.com

To find out more about
Charlie and Lola visit
charlieandlola.com